MEAT-EATING PLANTS

Avery Willebrant

REAL LIFE readers™

Rosen Classroom™

New York

Published in 2009 by The Rosen Publishing Group, Inc.
29 East 21st Street, New York, NY 10010

Book Design: Michael J. Flynn and Dan Hosek

Photo Credits: Cover © Hannu Liivaar/Shutterstock; pp. 4, 5 © Norman Chan/Shutterstock; p. 6 © David Huntley/Shutterstock; p. 7 © Thomas Mounsey/Shutterstock; pp. 8, 9 (left) © chai kian shin/Shutterstock; p. 9 (right) © Regina Chayer/Shutterstock; p. 10 © Maslov Dmitry/Shutterstock; pp. 10–11© Steve Hopkin/Taxi/Getty Images; pp. 12–13 © FloridaStock/Shutterstock.

ISBN: 978-1-4358-0077-9
6-pack ISBN: 978-1-4358-0078-6

Manufactured in the United States of America

CONTENTS

GROSS!

Did you know that there are more than 600 kinds of plants that eat meat?

Most meat-eating plants eat bugs.

Some meat-eating plants eat **tadpoles**, frogs, small birds, and even rats!

Unlike most plants, meat-eating plants grow well in soil that's low in **nutrients**.

The plants get nutrients from the meat they eat.

This meat-eating plant looks pretty on the outside. The inside, however, doesn't look as pretty!

Venus flytraps, like the one shown here, are sometimes called snap traps. Their leaves snap shut when touched.

VENUS FLYTRAP

The Venus flytrap eats all kinds of bugs.
The plant's trap is really two leaves.
When a bug lands on the leaves,
they snap shut.
There are thick hairs on the edges of the
leaves that trap the bug inside.
The more the bug moves, the tighter
the flytrap gets.

It can take 10 days for a Venus flytrap to eat the bug.

PITCHER PLANTS

Pitcher plants have leaves shaped like jugs. The leaves are **slippery**. Bugs fall or crawl into the leaves and can't get out.

The leaves have juice at the bottom. The juice slowly eats the bugs.

The pitcher plant on the left grows on a vine. The plant on the right grows out of the soil.

There are over 100 kinds of pitcher plants.
Most are small and only catch bugs.
The largest pitcher plant can catch
frogs and rats!

SUNDEWS

Sundews have many tiny **stalks**.
These stalks make a sticky juice.
Bugs think the juice is food.
They get stuck when they touch it.

When bugs try to get free, the sundew curls up. Bugs get covered with juice and die. Then, the stalks make another juice that eats the bugs.

PLANTS IN DANGER

Most meat-eating plants grow in **wetlands**.
Today, these plants are losing their homes
as people destroy wetlands.
Why should we try to keep meat-eating
plants safe?

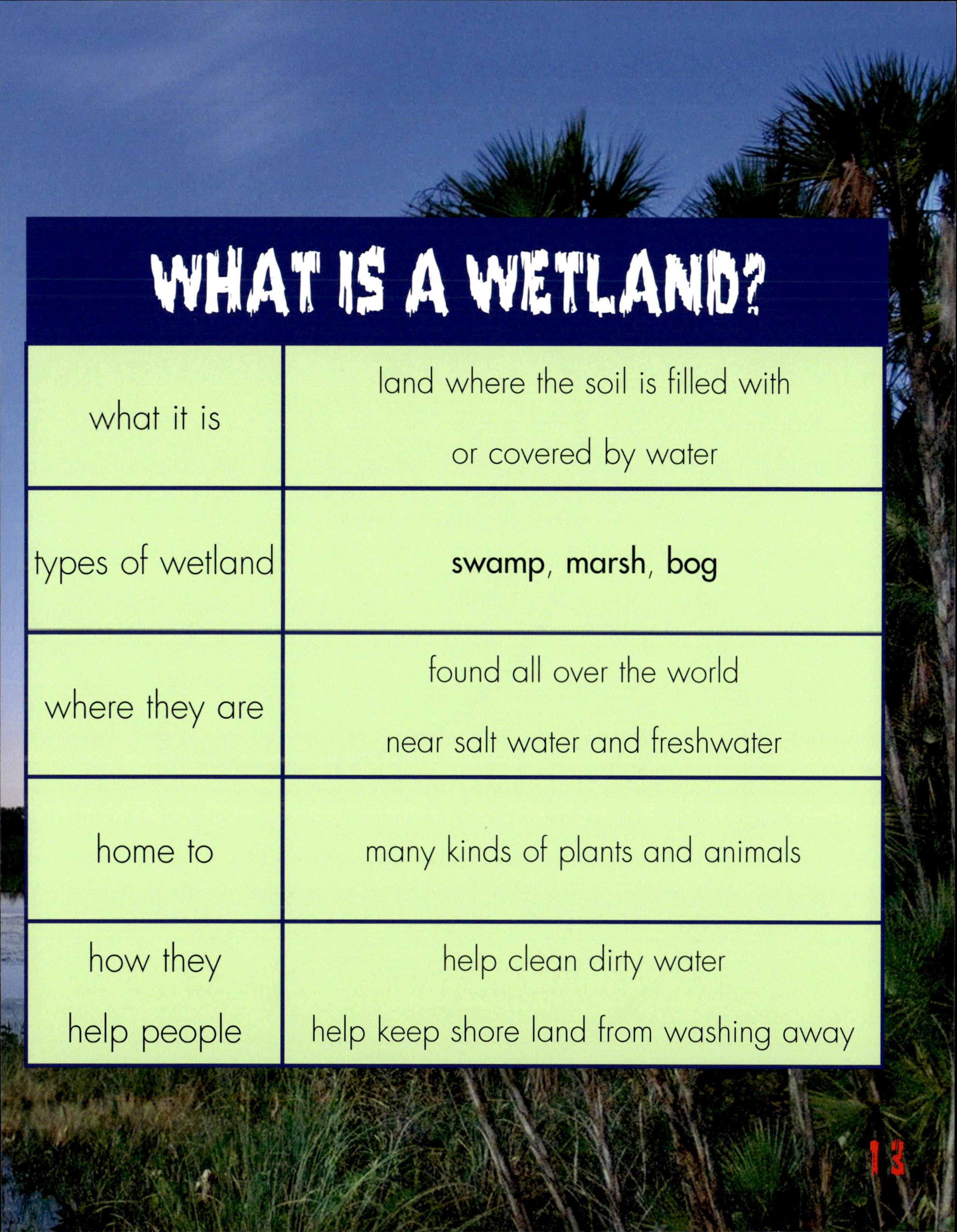

WHAT IS A WETLAND?

what it is	land where the soil is filled with or covered by water
types of wetland	**swamp**, **marsh**, **bog**
where they are	found all over the world near salt water and freshwater
home to	many kinds of plants and animals
how they help people	help clean dirty water help keep shore land from washing away

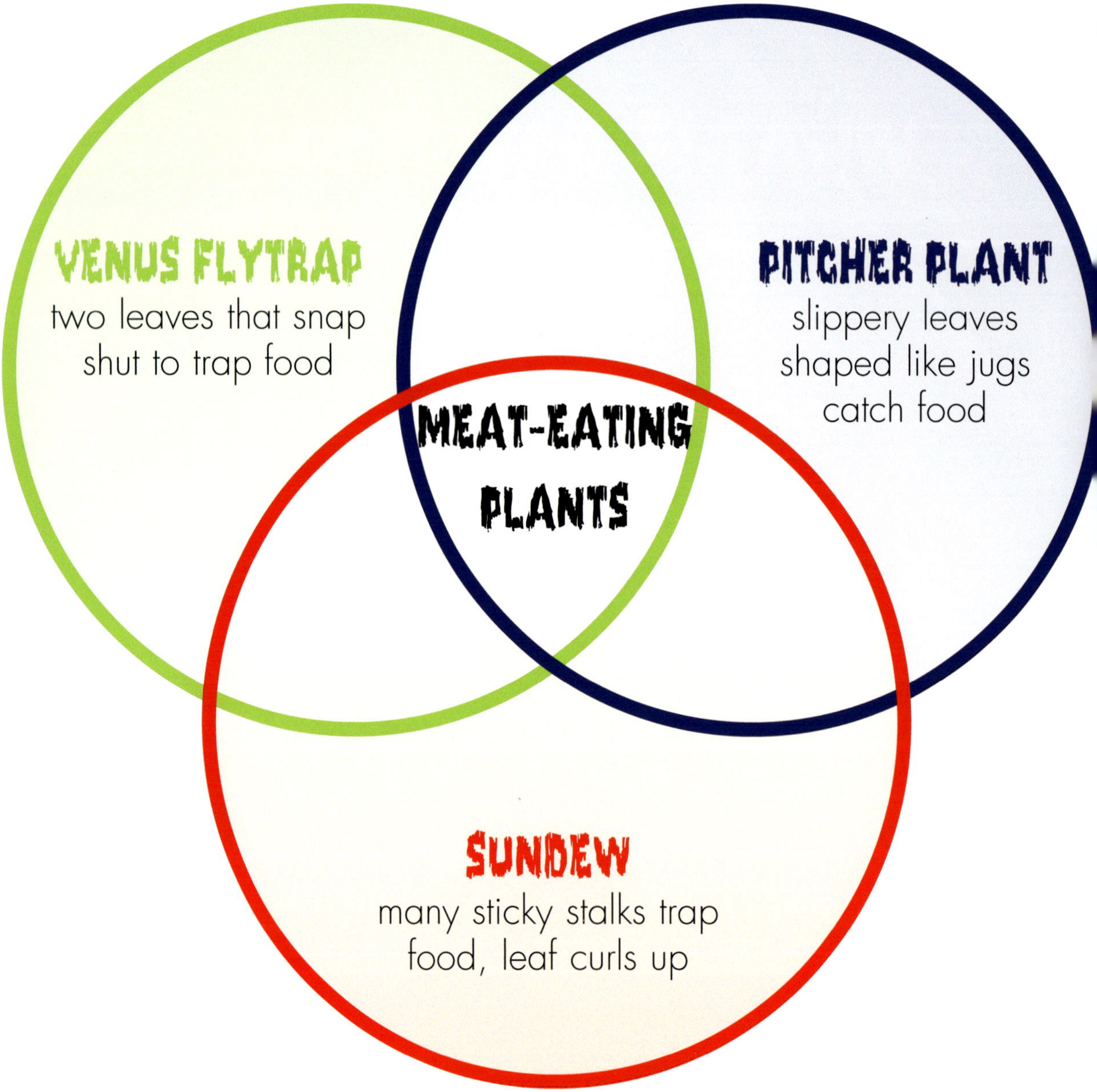
VENUS FLYTRAP
two leaves that snap shut to trap food
PITCHER PLANT
slippery leaves shaped like jugs catch food
MEAT-EATING PLANTS
SUNDEW
many sticky stalks trap food, leaf curls up

GLOSSARY

bog (BAWG) Wet soil with a lot of dead, rotting plants.

marsh (MARSH) An area of soft, wet land with grasses.

nutrient (NOO-tree-uhnt) Something a living thing needs to live and grow.

pitcher (PIH-chur) Jug.

slippery (SLIH-puh-ree) Causing something to slide or fall.

stalk (STAWK) A long, thin part of a plant.

swamp (SWAHMP) A wetland with a lot of trees and bushes.

tadpole (TAD-pohl) A baby frog or toad that looks like a fish and lives in water.

wetland (WEHT-land) An area where the soil is filled with or covered by water.

INDEX

Due to the changing nature of Internet links, The Rosen Publishing Group, Inc., has developed an online list of Web sites related to the subject of this book. This site is updated regularly. Please use this link to access the list: **http://www.rcbmlinks.com/rlr/meat**